Zephyr

The Writers' Meraki

Book Squirrel Publication

Zephyr

Book*Squirrel* Publication

Regd. Under MSME Act.

"ZEPHYR"

By: SABA & KANISHKA

ISBN: 978-98-89557-22-0

Language – ENGLISH & HINDI

1st Edition

Formatting: MUSKAN SHAH

Cover: Mr.Ash

Zephyr

<u>ACKNOWLEDGEMENT</u>

We, compilers of this Anthology ,thank everyone in the Scribe team who helped Saba and me to complete this book. Special thanks to our promoters: Priyadarshini, Kirtesh, Shiwalika and few others who worked along with us for completing this book.

Compiling a book is harder than we thought and more rewarding than we could have ever imagined. None of this would have been possible without the contribution of co-authors. All 41 co-authors and their pieces are the essence. We thank Ashutosh Das and also "Ink and pen"writers community for giving us the opportunity to compile a book.

We are eternally grateful to each and everyone who're the part of this anthology. We take this opportunity to appreciate the publishing team who guided us till the end of this book.

Thank you

<u>INTRODUCTION</u>

Air is so soothing; without it we are nothing; expression of our heart is the same as the wind. Memories dispatch gently or showers upon stormingly .

"Zephyr" is an anthology in which the writers have poured out their experience and unexpressed feeling about someone or something .

Each piece is the part of poet's heart, just like zephyr they are; nostalgic, impulsive, gloomy, silent and or appreciating.

'Ink and pen' is a community for writers where they can share their ink , get appreciated for their 'heavy heart' and or gratitude ,and learn from each other. We organize online contests and award the best ones.

It's all based on perspectives ,for not everyone has same sight of perfection;

They have quality writers in their community who really ink their hearts out with full dedication for writing.

Those who yearn to join them contact them through instagram : @Ink_and_pen9

COMPILERS

SABA

AND

KANISHKA

<u>COMPILER – SABA KHANUM</u>

SABA KHANUM IS A TWENTY YEAR OLD
POETESS HAILING FROM ANDHRA PRADESH,
INDIA.

PASSIONATELY PENNING DOWN EMOTIONS
SINCE ©2018 . SHE IS A PUBLISHED CO- AUTHOR
IN 10+ ANTHOLOGIES, FROM BOTH NATIONAL
& INTERNATIONAL PUBLISHING HOUSES
UNDER THE PEN NAME _@ poetsregiment

CURRENTLY PURSUING MEDICAL SCIENCES
FROM RAJIV GANDHI UNIVERSITY OF HEALTH
SCIENCES

PROFESSIONALLY A DOCTOR IN MAKING.

A NATURE LOVER,

A PSEUDO PHILOSOPHICAL WAFFLE ,

AN ENIGMATIC PSYCHE ENTANGLED IN
BETWEEN WORDS,

AN INTROVERT

FIRMLY BELIEVES IN PLATONICITY.

AND LIBERTY OF SPEECH

YOU CAN READ HER THOUGHTS

FROM THE FOLLOWING BOOKS

"Resilente pen" _ by Fanatixx publications

"Eden of memories" _ Bishara publications

"Shades of heart" _ Bishara publications

"Feelings beyond infinity" _ four clover publications

"Undaunted souls"_ Reasons and laughter publications

"Illusion "_ Bishara publications

"Vaani : The sound of silence " _ Bishara publications

"The view of tiny writers towards infinity world "_
Reasons and laughter publications

"This is us" _ witches n pink publications (International)

"The world on trial : The earth's grand vengeance "
_witches n pink publications (International)

"Ambient heights" _ Ambient heights publications
(International)

Zephyr

Misplaced devotions _ Ambient heights publications (International)

"Writers unite"_ Four clover publications

Published Author to the book, Orenda : The writers league supported by bishara publications .

EMOTIONAL MISER

Hoarder of Emotions

Yet, A Miser

Who Spends It in Smaller Proportions

Partially a Broken Sapien

Controlling Emotions

Before The process of Domination begins

Picturising Negativity Beforehand

So That When Negativity Hits

It Doesn't Shatter Me Anymore

And I'm Intact Unbreakable

I Live Miles Away From Attachments

Bonds & Promises of Forever

Expectations Are Venomous

Served By Loved Ones

Intended To choke you

Where You Breathe Death

Zephyr

Expectations Bring Temporary Joys

Leaving Behind Permanent Scars

If The Same Remains Unfulfilled

It Aches, Suffers, Trembles

Here in The "Heart"

A Thunderstorm Heard by None

A Volcano Eruption Felt by None

But Within You

Being Paranoid, Where I Trust None

Being Pessimist, Where I Fail To Acknowledge

Goodness

Over Suspicious, Protective & Conservative

Only way to Ward off the Hitches Which Life Throws
Sporadically

Prioritising oneself First

Acknowledging Self Respect Keeping up Self Esteem

For You Cannot Please Everyone Out There

At Times Confusions Hit Me Hard

Zephyr

In Process Of Overcoming

The Trials & Temptations

Have I Transformed Myself?

Into Someone, Which Is Not Me

A Humanly Automated Machine?

I Choose Not to Acknowledge Vehemence

Everyday I Run Miles for Myself

To Escape From Myself

There's Always an Ongoing Battle In My Mind

I Divert Myself into Innumerable Directions

I try keeping Myself On Track

The Moment I Stop I'm Caught

The Waves Of Emotions Within Would Engulf Me

I Would Be Trapped

Which Would Be the Last Thing

I Would Expect From Myself

Zephyr

Turning Into A Dark Triad

A Pseudophilosophical Waffle

An Enigmatic Psyche Entangled Amidst Words .

_©Poetsregiment

REALMS OF IMAGINATION.

A weird, irresistible feeling

Which takes me back into times

Makes me explore into ancient times

Like I've been a part of Era

Where Monarchy survived

A weird irresistible feeling

Like I've stepped into dense woods

With green bushes aligned in irregular fashion

A star lit sky with

Moon close to its horizon seemed

Like it's approaching closer and closer

Towards me

Oak trees besides me looked like

A boogeyman in disguise

Who is staring at me from Behind

Following me

Waiting for me to turn

Zephyr

So that it can scare me off

Wolf's were now howling to the new moon

Turning my fears into tears

I ran until my feet were numb and swollen

Only to find myself into woods denser than before

My stubborn legs were held by undetermined forces

Compelling to make a move forward

With every move I found myself closer to the giant
mountains

A sudden white beam of light

With intensity so high that my retina couldn't picturise

An unusual, unfamiliar voice echoing striking my
eardrums "comeee to mehh"

Despite adrenaline levels reaching heights

Sweating trembling feeling blue and grey

The inner me holds grip on curiousity

Continues heading forward, towards the dense woods

Zephyr

The predomination of stronger intensity

Of weird irresistible feelings

Continue the more I navigate

In order to reach the conclusion,

My soul starts decoding

With a deep breathe,

Closed eyes

I felt the feeling a little more deep

than before

Opening my eyes to rename the weird irresistible feel as
a " desperate Relic"

Innumerable questions striking

Perpendicular to my forehead

"Is my soul in Quest of something, which escaped
unfulfilled in the past life "?

"Something which made a move competedly to be a part
of my present "?

"And destiny is favouring it, by easily gliding situations
which I'm unable to crack through "?

Zephyr

More a less like a jigsaw puzzle where every piece
correlates with the other

"Why do I have a strong feeling about incidents
happening in present are not new to me " !

May be I've felt this, way more earlier

With each question leaving a deep groove of curiousity
in my subconscious mind

Neither a 'yes ' nor a 'No' would set free these lines from
question marks

Few things are better if left unsaid

For not all truths are meant to be revealed.

__© poetsregiment.

CO-COMPILER - KANISHKA

A 17 year old girl named Kanishka, started to ink down her silence two years ago. She's from Jabalpur, MP. Her poems got published in International poetry books 11 times, in US and UK. She represented India and won the "International bloggers fest 2018" organised by 'Fuzia', one of the biggest community of women. Her poetry was one of the top 100 poems, worldwide, in 2018, and she also got 'an elite writer' status in Poets yearbook 2018. Her debut poetry book named "Melancholy Smile" launched recently on 31st October,2019.

She believes "If good things aren't happening to you then you are that good thing ought to happen to others".

Insta handle : @Untitled_ruin

COUPED LAMPOON

She an alumna of life 17

Who hanker assess of her in teens.

But the reflection was woe-begon

Which deep inside clashed in ben!

It's nothing now; she 'as belittle ;

Although acceptable,

they hold larger part of her life .

She closed her eyes to save that piece

That was prestigious as her heart...

Then one dawn a thought cracked

And walked upon —

"Why are you bemoan?"

Reminded her of behove, dressed on.

She hates how they've drifted apart

But again she thought you were ally,

Ugh! Obviously it was and is wrong to say.

If they don't make an effort to keep her

In their lives then who's she

Zephyr

And why only she should try?

Putting all this aside, cleaning her study side,

"Why to think alike when it's my step

Towards my life".

Since then she mingle more with them

—intentionally

While they lampoon, teasingly.

Taking it as a round of applause

She guide her pen to coup and drop.

©Misskanishka

MEMORIES

Memories are weird contradiction,

They kill you and keep you alive

At the same time.

Everything is blurred;

Everytime you lay on bed

The flash back hits you.

Your first crush, your 1st wish,

Your best friend, once who was.

Everything that you have been through.

You don't understand

Where does the time go?

You don't.... You just don't know.

You don't know what you feel ,

At a moment you smile and then weep.

You feel insane, tied up with chain.

Nothing is clearly visioned in brain

But whenever you go through

The memory lane

You suffocate in pain.

Zephyr

Memories are nature's game

And are real demons,

Memories are sometimes fake heaven.

©Misskanishka

<u>CO-AUTHOR</u>

TITHI JOSHI

Hailing from Jabalpur (Madhya Pradesh), is an eighteen years old girl who recently completed her schooling .

She will now be pursuing a career in computer science but also has a keen interest in writing poems and drama in both English and Hindi languages.

She acclaims that the inspiration for her poem is inspired from the cordial shared between her family members who indeed are her greatest supporters.

NOT WORTH LEARNING

Few faces

We forget, all they had graces.

Now may be there,

May not be tommorow,

This path shows us all to sorrow.

Never we think,

This journey isn't endless,

Ends for now, makes us breathless.

Hand in hand now,

May not further be reached,

But this is not what we are preached.

How we celebrate birth,

But death, for us, is not that Worth,

For it seems to be disturbing.

Watching moments turning into memories is not worth
learning.

©Tithi

CO-AUTHOR

RAGNIL PATEL

Ragnil Patel is a LOGOPHILE.

Also known for his authenticity in

Dark and grey sense of penning.

#OLEANDER

Ig:- devious_ambivert

BRITTLE GLANCE

The sound had a reminiscence

Brittle was the word.

Joyous was my pain.

As it's all about "A PEARL".

Broke me for once,

Not just once for every instance.

Broke my smile.

The one intact for long.

Broke my every ounce,

Taking all of me along.

The narrative pleasure is last to seek;

Wait for the time and glance to leak.

The glare was an emotion to reach

"MAGNIFICAL" was the word.

Though it broke me away;

My heart was last at heard.

Zephyr

It's imprint to preserve

It's a reincarnation drop.

The relief of having "A FRAME".

At a price of losing hope.

It did break me

Not to be beside

The glance that was brittle

But, to live aside.

PEARL TO IT'S CEASE

RIGHT ABOUT TO FALL

I WATCHED

ABIDE BY BOUNDS,

UNDENIABLE TO CALL.

GOD,

"I WISH RELIVING THE

BREATH-TAKING MOMENT

ONCE AND FOR ALL."

©Ragnil Patel

<u>CO-AUTHOR</u>

SHIBANGI DAS

She is currently doing her graduation in zoology hons.

She is a bookaholic ambivert.

Life seems a puzzle to her and writing is helping her to solve it out.

A voracious reader, aims to change the world with her flowing ink.

CONFUSION

She wanted to share everything with her yet she hesitated. She thought if she gets her wrong and what if her 'bit of freedom' would get snatched away again? But today a strong urge came over her and she opened her bottled feelings in front of her. But little did she knew that what she thought earlier would come true and she would be bruised with heart wrenching taunts. When everyone gossiped in her class about their mothers and phrases such as ' Mommy is my bestie', it was just a dream for her which will remain unfulfilled for her forever.

She wanted her daughter to be the best in academics and she makes every possible effort to keep her away from the close friendships and love that comes in the category of nonsense stuff in her opinion. But when she listened her today, hopelessness and anger rode over her and made her abusive for that moment. She didn't wanted to as she pondered over that moment later but what else could she do. She didn't wanted her daughter's life to be ruined as hers had. But isn't it like that everyone's life isn't disastrous, so why keep one away from the problems one should face so that it could make her stronger and stronger day by day?

And the mother and daughter both confused, built a bridge of confusion between them that they were not able to cross ever.

©Shibangi

CO-AUTHOR

PRATEEK JAIN

Prateek Jain's tryst with writing happened to satiate the urge for expressing his experiences, observations and imaginations. Along with writing poems, he also likes to read books, write & read articles and cook food. For living he works as legal officer with an insurance company to fuel his interests & hobbies.

THE JOURNEY OF A LEAF

Shed by mother tree,

The wind picked me,

Went to the city,

Felt really pity,

Over the condition of human,

Turning more & more inhuman,

Dropped into a river,

Though it was more like a sewer,

Suffocated by sand,

Washed to ocean at the end,

Covered in oil slick,

Will die anorexic!

©Prateek Jain

<u>CO-AUTHOR</u>

SHIPRA KHANNA

She's a chairperson of NGO,

loves doing constructive work for the society,

Likes writing in free time.

GENTLE BREEZE

Swiftly the breeze blows

Flowers moving with the speed,

Of the breeze

Seems all creation

Is loving it:

Ripples forming

In the lake

Weather so cool:

Cloudy and lively

Breeze blows;

All flow, with the blow...

©Shipra

CO-AUTHOR

ANMOLDEEP

"Anmoldeep, a poet and a student, happily engaging in her realistic fantasies of the mind, is still on the voyage of learning the proper essence of poetry. Her educational background has given a great boost to her enthusiasm for writing, especially in poetic field. She always ensures that her readers get the best out of her words."

A BATTLE WITH THE WIND

I stood there, in muted rain,

with umbrella atop my face,

waiting for the traffic lights, to give permissions, and
retire my place.

Green soon coruscated, crowd traversed,

the unchallenging wind did blow,

but as I trod, along the barred cross,

the wind started its brawl.

It tugged my gamp, once and twice,

thrice and many a times,

two vigours, pulling opposite, none wanted to pause.

My crisp formals, dampened, but I didn't care a whit,
because I was engrossed,

wrestling, my own battle with the wind.

©Anmoldeep

<u>CO-AUTHOR</u>

NAINA BHATIA

This is Naina Bhatia,25 year's old punjabi girl from
Raipur Chhattisgarh.A rookie writer and a feminist too.
It's her first anthology. She is also a full time professor
but still loves to pen down her daily life experiences.You
can read her more writings at YourQuote.

"Lavleen kaur"

SOCIETY'S GIRL

Let her build her own castle,

Don't arrest her for just the society's

Legal certification of sex,

Or their so called marriage,

Let her decide her own destiny,

She hasn't born only to satisfy

The society's image & expectations,

Or their so called

Rituals or traditions!

©Naina

<u>CO-AUTHOR</u>

MANSI SUNIL KAVALE

MANSI SUNIL KAVALE IS A TWENTY YEAR OLD POETESS HAILING FROM MAHARASHTRA , INDIA. SHE IS PENNING DOWN HER THOUGHTS SINCE ©☐2012 AND ON PAGE _MSWRITES_POETIC_VIBES SINCE ©☐ 2018.

SHE IS CO- AUTHOR IN UPCOMING INTERNATIONAL ANTHOLOGY "BEST 1000 POEMS ANTHOLOGY".

CURRENTLY PERSUING THIRD YEAR BIOTECHNOLOGY FROM PUNE UNIVERSITY.

SHE IS PASSIONATE ABOUT PHOTOGRAPHY LOVES ACTING ; SHE WAS A LEAD ACTRESS IN MANY SHORTFILMS.

YES! I AM A GIRL.

Saniya is winning those medal on medal

Why still society says 'no girl child'

It's really a difficult riddle...

We are not terrified; we also have voice

Let us do what we want ; we have choice.

Dear society , let us fly

Don't stained us with blame ;

Just accept this fact that

boy and girl are all ways same..

Let's wake up the mind nd thoughts;

Give our life a new curl ;

I am not ashamed, instead proud

Beacuse yes ,I am a girl .

©Mansi

<u>CO-AUTHOR</u>

BASHARATH FATHI

He was born in India and his journey of writing started in Canada, when he came across the poem —"why I didn't wrote my first poem" by the 13 year old kid. That made him to express his feelings, emotions based on his perspectives.

His first anthology was "Musings of inner souls" and second was "Resilient pen".

You can check out his more work at YourQuote - Basharath fathi.

KISS ME AGAIN

Kiss me again

Not for the feelings or lust

But for the part that I never been...

Recite me again

Not for the part that I never been

But for the solutions that I never got credit...

Worship me again

Not for the inspirational thing

But for the negative thing that turned your life in a
positive way.

Hate me again

Not for the cruel intentions

But for the deeds that was a ruler until your perspective
made it a sin.

Zephyr

Love me again

Not for the terms and conditions of our loyalty program

But for the commitment of hidden loyalty that applies
within family members.

©Basharath

Love me again

<u>CO-AUTHOR</u>

YASEEN SHAIK

Hailing from Tirupati , His name is Yaseen Shaik

Currently fixing smiles (budding dentist)

also he loves to pen all the voiceless expressions

According to him the silent souls have meaningful
poetries!

BLURRED

After so long

He found her pic

It's blurred ,

He thought it's

Because of his glasses

Irony is,

It's because of his eyes

Which were,

Wet with tears !

TITLE : S/o

You are a Businessman? You are a doctor ?
You are an CEO ?
Whatever you might be today ,
But nothing will give better definition
To your name without s/o
Don't be proud because you are famous
Be proud to be s/o

©yaseen shaik

<u>CO-AUTHOR</u>

VANEESRI KAUL TYAGI

An ambitious writer from Gurgaon, Vaneesri Kaul Tyagi is a fashion student and shades speak out loud to her. Her eyes often rest upon the things that do not exist and she tends to pen those down too, apart from writing about her life experiences, love, and the greys. Her observation works without any boundaries in her imagination, and she likes to scribble about her own world more than the one that resides around her.

Her ink flows in a poetic, as well as a descriptive manner, and her ideas are open to be a participant in the upcoming anthologies or any other collaborative projects.

Instagram: @honeyberrrries

POEM

Every night,

It's just you

And me,

And all my life

Is on my lips.

But you put

A cigarette,

Between them

And tell me to wish for something,

Every time I exhale.

- all the times I almost kissed you.

©Vaneesri Kaul Tyagi

<u>CO-AUTHOR</u>

DHIVYA

She is Dhivya, a south Indian,

who loves art and literature to the core.

"If I could express everything, I wouldn't have started
writing!"

DEAR SOULMATE

When my heart wanted to crash,

She set my worries aside in a trash,

Never knew she would become this close,

Her sweet surprises always made me froze,

Disasters came like a storm,

She was always there to make me calm,

Her shoulders gave me comfort,

She melts my heart without an effort,

She knows how messy and rude I could be,

Yet, she showed how strong I would be.

Yes, she is my soulmate!

©Dhivya

CO-AUTHOR

PRIYADARSHINI NATH

She's an 18 year old poetess hailing from West Bengal, India. She is an extremely talented girl, doing 'Major in English' from Calcutta University. Books give her utmost pleasure ; she indulges in drawing in her spare time, when she is not penning down her thoughts.

She is a nature enthusiast and animal lover and draws inspiration from them.

EXHAUSTED DESIRE

Slumber is teasing my eyes

But tears are not easing my cries,

My lips have become infinitely dry,

And my ears hate listening to others sly.

Yet my brain is processing this lie-

That I am nasty and wry

Then I....

Build up courage in

small heart of my.

And so my feet leaps up in sky,

But cannot go very high!

As my broken wings deny-to fly;

In this vast expanse of sky.

©Priyadarshini Nath

<u>CO-AUTHOR</u>

SUMIT SAHA

An 18years old guy who has cracked NDA and now he is preparing for his SSB interview now. He wants to become an Air Force Officer. He loves to share his feeling with his poems. And he loves to write and fight with his hands.

He is crazy about cricket and kabaddi.

AN ABORTED CHILD

Both were mature enough to know the fact,

They did a mistake which left an impact.

Was it love or just having fun?

When they were asked, they answered none!

She came to a conclusion

To have an RU-486.

Without thinking about that child.

How did they conflict?

That 2 Months of paid relationship

Became a significant role!

They wanted to just have some fun,

But they killed an unborn soul.

©Sumit Saha

<u>CO-AUTHOR</u>

VISHAKHA SHAW

She's Vishakha Shaw, a simple girl residing in Kolkata. She's pursuing B.Sc (hons.) degree in Physics from the University of Calcutta. Writing is neither her hobby nor her passion. It's her Addiction. She writes what her heart says. Writing gives her a sense of satiation and peace to both her mind and soul. Besides writing, she enjoys doing painting, listening songs and reading books. She's really very thankful to her parents for giving her this beautiful and comfortable life.

THE FIREFLIES

53

Fluttering fireflies were once shimmering stars,

Who wanted to be free,

Free to roam around in the sky

So they fell and began to fly !!

They dance in the dark nights making the nights look
fearless,

And so does the magical nights elevates the beauty of
fireflies !!

They light up the stars in my sky every night and warm
up my dim cold heart,

They illuminate my soul and sets it free,

Free from the bars of the society

So that I can fly with freedom

Emitting my own light of grace and pride !!

©Vishakha Shaw

CO-AUTHOR

ABHIGYAN SHRIVASTAVA

Abhigyan Shrivastava, a B.Tech undergrad in Information Technology at National Institute of Technology, Raipur is a passionate writer. Besides playing guitar, he also tries capturing nature in his camera as exquisitely as possible. He likes to portray his feelings through poems and short anecdotes.

I TRIED

I tried to live every single day,

I tried, didn't fail, so kept moiling.

Later to realize, 'twas all futile,

better not to live, if living for yourself.

I opened my arms, to give all I have

O hijos de Dios, come take it from me

But soon, very soon, 'twas barren again

Folks ain't the same, they used to be,

you will be used, till you choke and die.

What did a hammer achieve, cutting trees all its life?

Do what you're good at, is the essence of life,

then pass the carcass, off to this soil.

Good bye o traveller, you soul shall never die,

you made this world, a better place to live.

©Abhigyan

<u>CO-AUTHOR</u>

SWAPNIL SINGH

Instagram Handler : __agnoized__dreamer

"Co-author for The View of Tiny Writers and The Sacred Bond"

Compiler of the Book " *ORENDA: The Writer's League " & " *Melancholy : The Lost Person* "

He is a person who hustles hard. Writing isn't an inborn talent but a procreated passion in him. From the agony, he came to the ecstasy he belongs. He is a person of value and deep affection. Deep down in his writing, you will find a 'you' and will stay there forever . "

AT SOME POINT

You need to deal with yourself. However not simply your heart but rather your brain and your body, as well, needs your understanding and care, too needs your adoration and delicacy, focuses on yourself, gives yourself what you have to stay healthy.

To purge your psyche and body— to free it of any contamination. Your heart is the blossom. your psyche is the dirt and your body is the stem. everything that makes you-you is associated and all that you take in.

© Swapnil

<u>CO-AUTHOR</u>

JESSICA

B.A 1st year student from Jabalpur ,Madhya Pradesh.

She loves writing and reading.

Her hobbies are painting and photography.

She's having a strong desire to become a writer.

TRUTH

The truth they know

May hurt you more,

The truth they don't know

May kill you whole.

The words they hear aren't true,

But helpless you can

No longer reach your voice

To tell the truth.

It seems unfair as

Your wishes become your death,

But you still stay alive

With the lifeless soul

Underneath your chest.

©Jessica

<u>CO-AUTHOR</u>

KANAK KESHARWANI

14 years old girl from Jabalpur, Madhya Pradesh.

She loves to sing, dance and write.

Her aim is to become a writer Inspire others.

TEACHER

A teacher who fills students' life ,

With full of colours .

From darkness they bring ,

Our life into brightness.

A teacher is God ,

Who show us our goals ,

Who introduce us with ourselves ,

Who tells what we are ,

Who tells how to co-operate ,

Who tells the meaning of life,

Who tells the importance of school life ....

They are our influencer ,

Who inspire us to do well ,

A teacher is a guide ,

Who mold us to crave pages.

Some teachers are unforgettable ;

For they leave their previous trace in our lives .

World teach us diamonds are precious than stones .

Zephyr

But a good teacher will make a stone,

more precious than a diamond .

Thank You for giving us enough knowledge ,

You are the precious gem of students' life.

Thank You for inspiring us ...

©Kanak Kesharwani

<u>CO-AUTHOR</u>

PROSARI CHANDA

Pursuing Masters in English Studies.

A bohemian, post puberty writer, been associated with indie filmmaking. Have written for a few anthology books, and hope to be a published writer one day.

POEM

Earlier I'd seen you

where the mountains grew purple

Just beyond Sunset!

As if a home lied there for us

for our truths to lay hidden

Golden his hair, like the color of sand be,

I see the sun die a slow death

Lighting up the horizon: The solemn waves lie
incarnadined.

I pull myself to those mountains- where the red sun
runners go

With each breath, I taste the sea better.

Closer to the horizon, my dreams sail deep.

©Prosari

<u>CO-AUTHOR</u>

KSHAMA

Kshama has written and published ten books.

She has received the Literoma achiever's award for her work as an author.

POEM

I want to be the reason of your smile; I want to be the solution
for your problems,

I want to cherish each moment we live, I will be on your side
through thick and thin,

I don't want to be in front of you or behind you; I want to walk
by your side,

All I aim is because of you and all you are is because of me,
we will never apart,

My sweetheart, my life, my hero, my love, my husband.

****

You protect me, you love me, and you help me,

You are my cushion, so gentle, so caring,

I am blessed with your unconditional love,

You forgive all my mistakes with patience,

You are my cook, my nurse, my teacher, I adore you,

You are a role model, I admire you, and I respect you,

Nobody is equal to you, thank you mom for everything,

You are a gift to me. I love you.

©Kshama

CO-AUTHOR

GOWRI

Gowri belongs from the southern part of India who is now pursuing her job in IT in Pune.

She loves reading and finds poetry in every little aspects of life.

She had been a part of an anthology named "Voice of Hearts" which was her first step towards the writing field.

She aspires to be a renowned writer one day. She has her own page of write-ups on instagram named "Itsy_Bitsy_Tales"

ME TOO

Fear filled in my head

the images flashing continuously

making me shiver and tremble

like I was a moth on fire.

Brave and strong that's who I should be

but here I am like a fragile bird

who is now scared to leave it's nest

just because of that incident.

For months I stayed in my shell

in search of the voice

that once roared like a lion

which is now muted.

It feels like I have lost my soul

it happened with me too.

I ain't a girl but a boy,

It's not safe to be one either.

©Gowri

<u>CO-AUTHOR</u>

BARSHA

Born on 6th January 2002, Barsha passed her high school from Barrackpore. She is presently doing her graduation in English Literature. She is a 17 year old promissing young poetess in the early stage of her maturation. If the morning shows the day then we may expect the emergence of a powerful pen in future from her.

NORTHERN LIGHTS

Wandering over the white snow,

reminds me of your smooth skins glow.

With each step I was getting closer to your heartbeat.

I gazed upon the sky.

Yes it's true , I saw you

Painting the night sky.

Aurora, I shouted with joy!

Your ability to shine in the darkest of all dark nights,
gifted you with the name for northern lights.

©Barsha

<u>CO-AUTHOR</u>

POOJA

Pooja is an aspiring writer from Mumbai, exploring the world beyond and penning it in words to bring out the very essence of it.

She loves writing contents, poems or micro stories on topics like love, life and any random situation or object that pulls her towards it.

She is a true dreamer and looking forward to participate in upcoming anthologies.

She can be reached out on her Instagram Page : poeticp7

OH MIND!

Oh Mind! You are so cunning and tricky!

Who always puts Heart trapped and twisted

You always seem to so be so lucky

But poor little Heart off goes busted

Oh Mind! You are so cunning and tricky!

Heart tries to follow her desires

To be finally free from all worries

But you put Heart's dreams on fire

My dear,

Reconcile with your dearest Heart

Just put an end to this heinous War

And weaving the thread of hopes

For Sure you will conquer the globe!

©Pooja Ashok More

CO-AUTHOR

SAYANTANI ROY

She is a literature student of the famous BETHUNE COLLEGE in kolkata. She is an absolute rational human being. She is a fantastic debatar, a very good speaker as well as a fabulous influencer. She is passionate about writing, it could be upon anything ,she just finds her way through it.She firmly believes that poetry is made up of pure happiness, pure souls and pure sorrow ,its a culmination of various emotions ,teachings and realism that manifests into a single thing.

I SWEAR!

With the shine in my heart,

I swear to light up the world, to the extent of prosperness
of ourselves!

With every inch of increasing happiness,

I swear to spread generosity, healingness and love.

With the sparkles of light,

I swear to enlighten up all the souls in a right path.

And with every sorrow,

I'll promise them a best day tomorrow.

With every fall of the rose petals,

I'll make sure to gift a bouquet of flowers...

And finally with a broken heart,

I swear to myself that I'll present myself a beautiful heart
again!!!

©Sayantani Roy

CO-AUTHOR

D. DAPUNII

D Dapunii is an IT professional who always see diversity as a beauty.

Outside his work, he love reading books and writing poems and quotes.

He is originally from Manipur, currently he lives in Mumbai.

"THE CHILD IS IN THE SHELTER HOME."

She kept the pain to herself.

So uncertain as rolling dice.

The fortune she hold fade so quickly.

Fill herself with sorrow and turmoil to the brim.

Her beauty in Marigold is heavily weary.

And she only know why?

Her grief multiple in her soul and she only endure.

Misguided and distorted by cruelty.

Was given the wine of lust in love.

Pleasure and pain in common cup.

Their headless fun and heartless pleasure blurred her
vision.

Adversity and Misfortune pile up like pyramid.

Their judgement too near and hand so far.

Their assumption so rot spit on her face.

Zephyr

No way left but to throw herself in ocean of tear.

Friends of lonely, whispers by fear.

Strengthen by a beam that come form broken window.

Goosebumps and heebie-jeebies as she hold the window
bar..

Her world within the four wall of the fence.

Should anyone read this!

Know there is a Child waiting for Love.

©D Dapunii

<u>CO-AUTHOR</u>

KSHAMAA. S

Kshamaa. S has been a little storyteller ever since she learned how to form sentences and now her voice is being heard by the world in the form of writings. An avid reader and an introvert her means of conversation is by words written. She hopes that one day the world can read her voice and relate to her. She can always be reached through Instagram : @hearts_that_bear_pain

THE GENRE I NEVER WROTE

The little smile across her eyes was all I ever wanted,

Before I walked away I knew tat it was granted.

The way she stood at the end of the street,

With a little box in her hand and a sack at her feet.

I knelt down beside her and asked her her name,

With a shy smile and a small bow she told me the same.

I held her hand and took her home,

From the little box I had I gave her my sisters old clothes.

She smiled and I knew I had done well,

I fed her and I took her to the orphanage by the rail.

I sent her there and promised to visit,

After my little sisters death this little girl begging on the
street was my only home..

©Kshamaa.S

<u>CO-AUTHOR</u>

ADBHUT

Is a poet, singer, songwriter and the author of an inspirational romance titled '#Social Love' which garnered immense love from the readers. He is currently travelling between places meanwhile writing his next book.

find everything about him on his website www.theadbhut.in and connect with him on his instagram @adbhuttt

SMELL I LIKE

That weird smell of wet mud in the park i used to play

with my nanny, Swati.

as my parents were too busy going to a reception or
attending meetings which stayed all night long,

just like Swati;

I knew my mother wouldn't know if I existed because
every time I called for her swati used to appear like a
jinny.

I was so used to her that my baby powder smell found
place in her body as well;

It wasn't very strange that i used to say 'okay mumma.'
to her and she wouldn't refuse but caresses my baby hair.

she used to sing me lullaby coming so close to my face
that I used to feel the tenderness even in her uneven
breaths;

was it a matter of concern that when swati left this world
in a miss-happening I was crying like I have become that
exact same baby which cried his heart out when he
needed warm milk and attention?

Zephyr

apparently no one used to come running except swati
like she knew what's happening inside my body—

well to be honest, no one was really there,

I'd still be crying like a baby but today also no one
would be there like swati.

All I am left are the smells which I remember and which
are her's only.

©Adbhut

CO-AUTHOR

SHIWALIKA SINGH SENGAR

She is Shiwalika singh sengar, who comes from the cleanest city of India I.e, Indore (MP). She's a simple girl rooted to her traditional values.She has done my bachelor's degree and currently pursuing CS (professional programme).She is passionate about different types of writings in hindi like poem's, shayri's ,gazal etc, since school days.She loves reading books like historical,mythological,novels etc.She has multiple hobbies like music, artistic works,exploring places,cooking etc.

Her Instagram write-ups handle is :- depths_of_hearts.

मंज़ूर

फिर हुज़ूर तुम्हारी रज़ा मंज़ूर करते हैं हम,

बिन कुसूर तुम्हारी सज़ा मंज़ूर करते हैं हम।

एक अरसे से जिंदगी हमने माना था तुझको,

तेरे तोहफ़े में अपनी क़ज़ा मंज़ूर करते हैं हम।

जन्नत-ए-बहारा ख़ुदाया तेरे कदमों में हो,

ये दोज़ख ये सर्द फ़िज़ा मंज़ूर करते हैं हम।

तुम रहो मशगूल तेरे इफ़्तखार के जश्न में,

अपनी बेज़ारी का ये मज़ा मंज़ूर करते हैं हम।

ग़र हराम है समीमी और वफ़ा ही अज़ाब है,

तो ये ताज़ीर,ये कस्र-अफ़ज़ा मंज़ूर करते हैं हम।।

©शिवालिका सिंह सेंगर

<u>CO-AUTHOR</u>

KARTIKEY SARASWAT

Kartikey Saraswat is a 18 yo boy , who couldn't tolerate heart break at age of 14 years and started penning down emotions and began carving them on pages . He believes by writing one can feel ease as how emotions remain immortal on piece of paper .

His writings were appreciated and encouraged by his friends and that's how his journey of writing began.

जवाब दोगी क्या?

एक सवाल है,जवाब दोगी क्या?

यूँ ही फलक तक मेरा साथ दोगी क्या?

होने लगें मंजिलें पूरी इस जहां की,

तो रोज जीने का नया ख्वाब दोगी क्या?

एक सवाल है,जवाब दोगी क्या?

खोने लगूँ कभी खुद के नशे में,

अपनी इन निगाहों की शराब दोगी क्या?

एक सवाल है,जवाब दोगी क्या?

कोई न हो साथ ज़माने में,

फिर भी साथ चलने को हाथ दोगी क्या?

एक सवाल है,जवाब दोगी क्या?

©Kartikey Saraswat

<u>CO-AUTHOR</u>

SHUBHRA SANAG

Shubhra sanag , belongs to Jhansi Up , pursuing masters in English literature from A.k.Mahavidyalaya Jhansi.

She found the writer in her when she was in 11 th standard .Her interest in writing started flying with the wings of birds.

When she joined the writer's community — "Your Quote". She is also passionate about crafting, singing, reading, writing lyrics etc,Because of writing she start loving nature, spirituality and the universe.

She wants to dedicate her life on woman empowerment, environment, underprivileged children.

"Let's do a happiness campaign,let's dissolve others pain and share a happy feeling."

तस्वीर

एक तस्वीर खींचनी है

उस गांव की जहाँ हम पले-बढ़े

लेकिन दोबारा कभी जा नहीं पाए;

एक तस्वीर खींचनी है,

वहां की जहाँ हमारी दो बीघा जमीन थी,

जिसमे हमारे दादा-दादी संग हमारा पूरा खानदान रहता था

उस देवड़ी की जहाँ हम बचपन में नहाया करते थे,

उस भूसे और खपड़ेल वाली छतों की जिस पर चढ़ कर हम सारे बच्चे

ताई के बने आम के अचार की बरनी में से अचार चुरा के खाया करते
थे।

एक तस्वीर खींचनी है,

उन चूल्हे पर बनी हुई बाजरे की रोटी की

जो दादी अपने हाथ से खिलाया करती थी।

उन सभी पलों की जिन्हे हम याद तो कर सकते है

लेकिन वापिस नहीं जा सकते,

उन धुंधली यादों की जो हम भूल चुके है।

©Shubhra

CO-AUTHOR

KIRTESH SHARMA

From Khachrod,dist, Ujjain.He completed his graduation in Electrical and Electronics Engineering from Rajiv Gandhi Prodhyogiki Vishvavidyalay, Bhopal. He writes in Hindi. He writes about life, society,love, seperation etc.

सफलता

असफलता की बारिश में सफलता की बूंदे ढूंढना है।

ज़िन्दगी तेरे आगे तो नहीं तेरे साथ साथ चलना है।।

है दूर सही पर उम्मीद नज़र आती है,ज़िन्दगी।।

है कई बार हार पर जीत नज़र आती है,ज़िन्दगी।।

है कई सवाल पर जवाब खोज लाती है,ज़िन्दगी।।

है पतझड़ पर सावन की बहार बन जाती है,ज़िन्दगी।।

आज अस्त है तो कल उदय है,

उदय-अस्त का मेल है,ज़िन्दगी॥

आज हार है तो कल जीत है,

हार-जीत का खेल है,ज़िन्दगी॥

जीत के है अवसर बेशुमार,

आज की हार से मत हार,ज़िन्दगी॥

असफलता की बारिश में सफलता की बूंदे ढूंढना है।

ज़िन्दगी तेरे आगे तो नहीं तेरे साथ साथ चलना है।।

©Kirtesh Sharma

<u>CO-AUTHOR</u>

AAKASH VISHNOI

Aakash vishnoi is a famous poet & a well known writer on yourquote.

He is a good singer and a very good guitarist. You can say that he is a person who is blessed with all the arts.

He has written more than 50poems.many of them are very popular.

He is co-author of many a anthologies.

The way he compose poems is really amazing.

You can read all his quotes on Google by searching aakash vishnoi quotes get connected with him on Instagram-

@aakash_vishnoi1

लोगों की समझ यहां कुछ और है

ना इंसान में रहे "ज़ज्बात-ए-पिन्हाँ" अब

ना ही फहम किसी के हालात-ए-जज़्बात की आकाश

लोगों की बनावट-ए-लिबास है कुछ और यहां

यहां लोगों के मिजाज़-ए-दिमाग कुछ और हैं

लोगों का सलीका-ए इतिंखाब बदल गया है अब

यहां लोगों की इबादत-ए-वफा अब कुछ और हैं

ना इंसान से गुजरती अब शब-ए-तन्हाई यहां

ना ही तन्हाई में कोई सूकन-ए-ज़हन आकाश

लोग तन्हाई में हैं कुछ और अब,

लोग साथ में हैं,तो कुछ और हैं।

ना रख जमाने से उम्मीदें तू ,

ज़ज्बात-ए-फ़हम की अब आकाश

तेरे बोल कुछ और हैं यहां, लोगों की समझ यहां कुछ और है।

©Aakash

<u>CO-AUTHOR</u>

ANAMIKA SINGH

She is from Delhi. She has completed her graduation from Delhi University and pursuing her post graduation from IGNOU. She loves to read not only literature but also about history and politics. She loves stories most.

She writes in Hindi, she writes nazms(नज़्म) poetries shayaris,one liners and two liners. She writes about society, love, separation etc. She writes whenever thoughts burst up in her mind and make her hustle for a pen and paper. She is a girl with lots of dreams and passion to fulfill them.

She lives her life on a quote,

"I want a life like fairytale,

I will make my own fairytale"

किरदार

सनसनी सी खबरें ढूंढते हो मुझमें

मैं कोई अखबार तो नहीं।

माना रंज-ओ-गम है जिंदगी में बहुत

मगर मैं बेज़ार तो नहीं।

मौहब्बत की उम्मीद रखते हो मुझसे

मैं शायर के अश्आर तो नहीं।

दिल तोड़ा महबूब ने मेरा

मगर मैं इससे शर्मसार तो नहीं।

बिखर गई है रूह मेरी

मगर मैं ज़ार-ज़ार तो नहीं।

समझ सको किरदार को मेरे ,

अभी तुम इतने होशियार तो नहीं।

©Anamika

<u>CO-AUTHOR</u>

GAUTAM YADAV

Welcome to the drappled path of his life:

A journey which was started in Agra, 19 years ago.

Two years back, this journey took an interesting turn to change his emotions into words in the form of writing.

And he knows, this book has the capacity to cherish and attract anyone to keep this hand sized book close as a small expression of his humanity.

Here you will be able to find each and every picture and description very melodious and the emotions of poets will make your days happier

मुसाफ़िर

खाली हाथ आया था मैं,

और खाली हाथ ही जाऊँगा,

पैसों की मुझे चाह नहीं,

पर नाम जरूर कमाऊँगा।।

अंधेरे को भी चीरूँगा मैं,

और उजाला भी पाऊँगा

मैं मुसाफिर हूँ साहब मंजिल तक पहुंच ही जाऊँगा।।

आँखे जितनी छोटी,

ख्वाब उतने ही ऊँचे रखता हूँ,

ज़िन्दगी के कड़वे सच,

मैं बड़े शौक से चखता हूँ।।

जितना मुझे गिराओगे,

मैं उतना ही ऊपर जाऊँगा,

मैं मुसाफिर हूँ साहब मंजिल तक पहुंच ही जाऊँगा।।

©गौतम यादव

CO-AUTHOR

KARTIKAYA BAJPAI

A volleyball player, A trekking enthusiast, A social worker...

I started penning down things because I found that's the best way of expressing yourself....

An ordinary person from City of Nawabs....

IG mera_safar_maa_se_maa_tk

एक ओर

एक ओर कहीं जग में, खुशियों ने बादल घेरे हैं।

एक ओर उसी जग में व्यास विकराल अंधेरे हैं।

एक ओर कहीं जग में, नदियां भी तो बहती हैं!

एक ओर उसी जग में, प्यासी भी जनता रहती है।

एक ओर कहीं जग में, खाना भी फेंका जाता है!

एक ओर उसी जग में, कोई भूखा ही सो जाता है।

एक ओर कहीं जग में, इन्सानों का मेला है!

एक ओर उसी जग में, कोई पड़ ही गया अकेला है।

एक ओर कहीं जग में, कोई मां को बोझ समझता है!

एक ओर उसी जग में, कोई मां के लिए तरसता है।।

©Kartikaya

<u>CO-AUTHOR</u>

DIVYA MANNEWAR

She lives in Jabalpur and has recently completed her graduation from RDVV University.

She likes to write and usually writes in hindi.

Particularly her domain for writing is about living the life and her views about society.

POEM

आग मुझमे भी हैं,

पर तेरे गुरुर जैसी नहीं,

लौ मुझमे भी है,

पर मशाल सी नहीं,

नफरत मुझमे भी हैं,

पर अंगार सी नहीं,

तेरी आग में गुरुर है,

पर हमारी आग कुछ सुकुन भी है ....!!!!

©Divya

CO-AUTHOR

PRAGYAN

Pragyan is a student of standard 11th and he had won the international movie making competition held in biggest school of the world. He had started writing quotation from standard 10th . He quote-》 I'm not perfect but stories are always better with a touch of imperfection♡!!

इरादे

कुछ इरादे जो इरादे से लगते नहीं

झुका देती हैं हमारी नजरें कभी

आगे बढ़ने देते नहीं

छीन लेते हैं वह हमारे खुशियों के पल

जो कभी अपनों ने पिरोया था

ए खुदगर्ज इंसान तुम्हें क्या पता

इन खुशियों को हमने कैसे संजोया था !!

©Pragyan

<u>CO-AUTHOR</u>

PRAGYA

Pragya is completing graduation from St. Thomas at Steel City Bhillai

She is a native of Chirmiri(a town in chhattisgarh).

Completed schooling from D.A.V public school (Navi Mumbai) and Aditya Academy(Kolkata).

She loves to pen out feelings and emotions in the form of words..

Fond of reading also.

She is a small town girl with high desires .

कुछ अपने पल

कभी-कभी लगता है कुछ पल अपने जी लू,

कभी-कभी लगता है यह दोहरे हिस्से वाले लोगों से दूर हो जाऊ,

कभी-कभी लगता है माँ के गोद मे बेफिकरा सो जाऊ,

कभी-कभी लगता है काश यह हर रोज़ की झूठी हँसी से बच
पाऊ।

....

बेवफ़ाई

सोचते -सोचते रह गया शायर कि कितने कम लफज़ो मे उसकी
बेवफ़ाई बयान करे,

आखिर महफिल मे उस बेवफ़ा का आना भी था।

©Pragya

<u>CO-AUTHOR</u>

ANISA KHATOON

A Logophile, is native of Patna, Bihar. She is a sensitive person who is working on becoming a stronger and a better person every day. She is pursuing PhD besides being a home maker. She believes that the toughest job in the world is to look after your family and still manages time to pen her emotions. She writes all that is locked up in her heart but in the hustle and bustle of life, failed to come on her lips. She loves to be in the company of her family and friends. She loves travelling because the experience makes her grow as a story teller. If you want to explore or contact this writer,then the links are below.

Instagram:- anisa.badar

QUOTES

(1) बदल लिया है मैंने ख़ुद को तेरे हिसाब से

अब तो आयीना देखना भी गावराह नहीं.!!

(2) कहते है वक़्त जार जख्म भर देता है,

लेकिन हर वक्त एक नया ज़ख्म भी तोह देता हैं.!!

(3) खामोश हु पर बेजुबान नहीं

चुप रह कर नाराजगी ज़तना भी एक अलग अदा हैं.!!

@Anisa

<u>COMPILER'S ENTRY</u>
<u>SABA KHANUM</u>

<u>ZEPHYR OF SECLUSION</u>

I scream my nerves out

Running out of words

To convey my depths

To set off the fire running in my veins

In search of vocabulary

Which can serve as veil

Letting off the caged demons free

Opening up my biggest fears

Inking them in closed books

Hiding them behind the closet

I fill my lungs with amusement

And feed my soul seclusion of

Zephyr!

_ © poetsregiment